T0375481

LEAVING
YESTERDAY

ROSA BAILEY

WESTBOW
PRESS®
A DIVISION OF THOMAS NELSON
& ZONDERVAN

WestBow Press books may be ordered through booksellers or by contacting:

WestBow Press
A Division of Thomas Nelson & Zondervan
1663 Liberty Drive
Bloomington, IN 47403
www.westbowpress.com
844-714-3454

Because of the dynamic nature of the Internet, any web addresses or
links contained in this book may have changed since publication and
may no longer be valid. The views expressed in this work are solely those
of the author and do not necessarily reflect the views of the publisher,
and the publisher hereby disclaims any responsibility for them.

Any people depicted in stock imagery provided by Getty Images are
models, and such images are being used for illustrative purposes only.
Certain stock imagery © Getty Images.

ISBN: 979-8-3850-1714-0 (sc)
ISBN: 979-8-3850-1715-7 (hc)
ISBN: 979-8-3850-1716-4 (e)

Library of Congress Control Number: 2024901174

Print information available on the last page.

WestBow Press rev. date: 4/16/2024

I

CHAPTER ONE

Melita Logan waited impatiently at the Market Street bus terminal. Her eyes scanned the stream of people flowing into the terminal. Sheila had promised to meet her at eight. It was now eight thirty. She spotted a woman waving to her from the top of the elevator who quickly crossed the floor and maneuvered around people to reach her.

"You made it." They embraced, and Sheila stepped back. "Let me look at you." She tilted slightly and looked Melita over with a maternal eye. "You still have that same innocent look." Sheila had married right after college. A husband, a career, and the responsibilities of married life had changed her. She looked older. She wore her hair in a short, sleek style, and her tailored coat and expensive boots and handbag added to her sophistication.

Melita felt tacky in her old blue jeans and down-filled jacket. "You look different," she said.

"I think it's my hair."

"No, it's more than your hair. You're a married woman now."

Sheila looked at the luggage Melita had brought. "You didn't bring much. The way you were talking, I thought you were bringing a truckload. This isn't bad at all. Frank can get it."

Sheila's husband of two years stood quietly watching the two of them and nodded in greeting. Melita knew him only through Sheila and his visits to their off-campus apartment during their college days. Even then he had been a young man of few words— quiet and thoughtful.

"Hi, Frank. It's nice to see you again."

They shook hands. He lifted the two suitcases, and Sheila picked up the garment bag. "We'll show you the city later," she explained. "It shouldn't be too hard for you to learn your way around. Christmas decorations are up, and the city looks pretty nice."

Melita followed them out onto Market Street, where Christmas decorations swayed in the night breeze. At one end of the street, City Hall stood bathed in white light. Across the street, the neon lights of a pornographic cinema beckoned. Melita looked away from the flashing lights.

"How do you feel?" Sheila asked.

"A little sad now that I'm here. I don't know if this was the right thing to do."

"Give yourself some time. You never know how things will turn out. This may be your town. You came at a good time. We can go to Center City at night and look at the decorations. And you must see Wanamaker's—especially the toy department. A train circles the whole toy department. And we can go to Gimbels and Strawbridge and Clothier. We're having Christmas dinner with my family and meeting at my cousin's house."

Frank drove up to a large apartment complex surrounded by trees and carefully manicured lawns. The two women walked quietly into the building while he parked the car. Sheila checked for mail, and they walked to the apartment door, which opened to reveal a room of brown and beige furniture accented with orange pillows and lush green plants. Sheila showed Melita the room that would be hers. It was large, bright, and sparsely furnished. "If you want to paint or buy furniture for yourself, you can. I'm not fussy that way." She was quiet for a moment and studied Melita's face. "I'm going to tell you something I never say to a woman: your face is beautiful. When we were roommates, I had no idea how beautiful you would become. You'll have a boyfriend in no time."

"Thank you, but I won't have time for a boyfriend. I need a job. Work is what I need."

Frank came into the room, set the luggage down, and left the women to their talk. Sheila sat on the bed and watched Melita unpack. "I'm so glad you're here." She sighed, and there was a sudden shift in her mood. Melita looked up from her unpacking. "Frank doesn't talk to me."

"I know. You told me the last time we talked."

"No. I mean he really doesn't talk to me. All he cares about is a hot meal after work and that television."

"Well, he never did talk a lot."

"But he's worse now, and last winter was terrible. He was so mean I thought an evil spirit was riding him. He wanted me to get pregnant. I teach, and I'm in graduate school. He works evenings at the hospital. Who's going to care for a baby? There's no one home. My mom was even pressuring me to get pregnant. I thought I was in hell or about to die and go there."

"How is he now?" Melita asked.

3

"He's calmer. But we still don't talk, especially not about children."

Melita put away the last of her things and slid both pieces of luggage under the bed. She sat on the floor near a vent and let the warm air rush over her feet. The two of them sat quietly, each in her private thoughts. The loneliness in Sheila's life and the loss in Melita's bound them together in a new and different way.

"What happened at home?" Sheila asked.

"I thought I was coping with Mom's death, but now I'm not sure." Melita looked thoughtful. "Dad was mean to me and my brothers after she died, and I felt like he didn't want us around anymore. I don't know what happened to him. He turned into this mean, bitter person, and I just couldn't take it anymore."

"Death does strange things to people."

"He acted like his loss was so much greater than his children's loss. We lost our mother. He can get another wife, but we can't get another mother." Melita felt the old hurt and anger that grief often brought her.

"Still, you have a lot of heart to come here. I could never leave my family and come to a new city. Do you know any other people here besides me?"

"I have cousins, but we don't really know each other. My uncle divorced their mother years ago when we were children, and they left town. I never saw them again."

"What if something happens and you can't stay here anymore?"

"I'll find someplace else to stay."

The thought of returning home didn't cross Melita's mind. Her mother's death had been hard on the family. It seemed the warmth and hope of the family had been centered in her. For

Melita, approaching young womanhood, the loss was especially painful. There were all those future moments to come without her mother. One day she would look through her wedding veil and feel a sudden, brief moment of loss. She would hold her firstborn and wish for her mother's presence. Death robbed her of those moments and her home. If only she had a sister, someone who together with her could remember. But there had only been brothers. Brothers who didn't know how to grieve and received no help from their only parent.

"Sometimes people don't know how to help one another grieve," Sheila said, breaking into Melita's thoughts. "And the hurt comes out in painful ways. When my cousin died, his mom started drinking."

Melita was unmoved. "Dad was just plain mean to us, and to think he's all we have now."

CHAPTER TWO

January was a busy time for the city. A new mayor was sworn in and wished well, and for the first time, citizens prepared to celebrate the life of Dr. Martin Luther King. His face adorned countless calendars, buttons, T-shirts, framed pictures, and pens. He was on posters and billboards. Melita had never in her young life experienced such public praise for a Black man.

She remembered the upheaval of the civil rights movement, and images of that time resurfaced in her mind amid all the praise for Martin. She remembered seeing Bull Connor on television and Emmett Till's battered and swollen face in a magazine photo. She remembered a white man standing beside the car Viola Liuzzo had driven when she was murdered—the car for sale like a trophy. She had studied the faces of the four girls murdered when a bomb exploded in their church. One of the girls had smiled in her photo, and Melita, all of nine years old, had thought she would have been a nice friend to have because her smile had been so sunny and warm.

Three civil rights workers named Cheney, Schwerner, and Goodman had been murdered during those years and buried in a shallow grave. A black bag held the remains of one of them and lay in an open casket on cushion softness the day of the funeral. There was a lot of water in the streets in those days from fire hoses that knocked Black men, women, and children off their feet as they protested against the pain and injustice of second-class citizenship. Police officers clubbed Black and white protesters and dragged them to police wagons. And sometimes Melita saw photos of white people grinning at all the suffering and hurt. Her mother never kept any of those awful days from her, despite her tender age. She wanted her to know and remember the sacrifices made and the blood shed to make her life better.

But this January was different. The citizens of Philadelphia and other cities seemed to search for healing and forgiveness. And America seemed to recognize at last the gift of Martin. Images of the past receded from Melita's mind. Like water leaving a shoreline, the images were washed out into a sea of reconciliation and healing.

CHAPTER THREE

Melita quickly joined a church that was impressive to her spiritually untrained eyes. On Sunday mornings, she enjoyed looking up at the angels adorning the sanctuary pillars. She could sit anywhere in the church and see them—something that comforted her. The church altar was made of smooth, milky marble, and the altar steps gleamed in the sunlight that streamed through stained glass windows. The dark wood of the pews was richly varnished, and the floors waxed to perfection. The large congregation required two Sunday morning services, and Melita preferred the early morning service. She had to get up at six in the morning to arrive on time but didn't mind. She dressed warmly and walked to the church in the snow, arriving with cold cheeks and a heart warmed by sacrifice.

The early morning service was full of older people devoted to fervent worship. They praised God with hands uplifted and arms outstretched. Some of them would call out praises and walk the sanctuary aisles thanking God and speaking of His goodness and mercy. Melita studied their faces and saw tears. In these unguarded moments she watched her elders and understood their gratitude without knowing how she understood.

It was in this church that Melita listened to the songs of her ancestors—songs that spoke not only of Jesus but of the longings of a people's heart. She heard the songs slaves created to inform, remind, and encourage one another. Feeling alone in the world, she believed her slave ancestors had loved her. Without knowing her, they had loved her through time and space. It was all there in the songs. People did not create such songs to be forgotten. The songs were gifts her ancestors left for her when they dreamed of freedom and indirectly of her.

This praise and song-filled service was very different from the later morning service, which was full of urban professionals and families who had escaped life in housing projects. This group of churchgoers had begun the long climb to middle-class propriety and prosperity. They were a quiet crowd and emotionally subdued in their worship. When Melita clapped her hands or said amen too loudly, she received disapproving stares, which made her feel self-conscious and bound.

The Sunday school director, sensing a tenderness in Melita that could touch children's lives, asked her to teach a class of very young children. But Melita refused. She believed a Sunday school teacher should live a clean life, and she had started going to nightclubs with Sheila and drinking hard liquor. But she did assist a deacon with visitation. Every third Saturday the two of them visited a nursing home where they read Bible verses and sang songs with the residents. Melita became friendly with Becky, one of the residents, and even made extra visits to see her. Becky had been a housekeeper for a wealthy white family and suffered a debilitating stroke while in their service. The family had placed her in the home and paid for her care. They visited regularly, and

Melita met them during one of her solo visits. They all hovered around Becky's bed, talking and smiling at her.

Becky used her hands and her smile to talk with them. As the weeks passed, Becky took out photos and letters from the family and tried to tell her about them. Somehow Becky came to believe Melita could reunite her with the family. Visits became stressful, and she didn't know how to stop visiting Becky without feeling she was abandoning her. On what became her last visit, Becky pulled Melita's clothes and tried to speak. She pounded her chest and shoved a photo of the family at her. Melita grabbed her Bible and left the room in a hurry, not bothering to relate the incident to a nurse. She decided Becky was losing her mind and felt a little hurt and rejected. When she told the deacon what happened, he tried to convince her to stay. "We don't have many members like you. You took the initiative to minister on your own," he explained. But Melita refused. No more sick people.

CHAPTER FOUR

Sheila's older sister found Melita a part-time job at the hospital where she worked. Melita was thankful to be employed but disappointed with part-time work. She had been careful to save some money while living at home and working in a small factory, and her savings would help until she found full-time work. The job consisted of filing and locating records for pediatric patients. It was the kind of work that had never appealed to her—sitting at a desk in an office. But it was nice to dress for work and eat lunch in the hospital's sunny atrium.

She finished each day's work and then rode the subway back to Mount Airy, determined to brave the fallout of Sheila and Frank's unhappy marriage. In the two years they had been apart Sheila had changed in more than appearance. She was no longer the easygoing, humorous, smiling friend she had once been. Melita remembered a lovestruck young woman who simply wanted to finish college and marry her childhood sweetheart. But this woman was gone.

"Frank and I used to sit and watch the trains sometimes. Simple things," Sheila told her. "He was so quiet and steady. He wasn't like the other boys. He didn't do the silly teenage things boys do. I could depend on him even in high school." And now this steadiness and dependability had become a boring liability.

Life with the two of them was one drama after another. Each weekend brought at least one fight complete with tears and threats. What did they fight about? Bills, relatives, money, her job, his job, how hard she worked, how he never did anything but watch television, how she didn't stay home with him and was always out somewhere.

When the fights really got out of hand, Frank would phone Ruth, who had been married to and deserted by Sheila's father. Ruth would come and talk to them in her best motherly tone about married life—its ups and downs. And she ended each talk with the classic line "After you've been married for a while, you'll understand what's really important." Calm would be restored for a few days. Then the same problems would rear their ugly heads all over again.

From what Melita could see, Frank did spend hours in front of his beloved television, and he was very quiet and unaffectionate. But when Sheila wasn't working or fighting with him, she spent long hours away from home visiting relatives and working on her master's degree. She tried to enlist Melita in her war against Frank, but Melita refused to join. She understood Sheila's frustration, but her father had warned her about married people: "They'll fight like cats and dogs and then be mad at you for interfering after they make up." Melita watched the marriage fray and prayed silently, hoping she wouldn't have a marriage like theirs.

One Saturday morning Frank knocked at her bedroom door. "Come have breakfast with me." His voice sounded pleasant enough, so Melita pulled on her robe and opened the door.

14

She assumed Sheila would join them too and walked into the kitchen expecting to see her. "Where's Sheila?"

Frank set a plate of food on the table. "She went out."

Melita sat down and watched him as he carried his plate to the opposite side of the table. "When is she coming back?"

"I don't know. She went shopping."

Melita prayed, raised her fork and then paused. "Did you make breakfast for Sheila?" she asked.

"Why are you asking me all these questions? Just eat."

"Did you make breakfast for Sheila?" Melita asked again.

"No. She always goes out too early." He seemed irritated. And that word—*always*—bothered her. Sheila didn't always do anything. Sometimes. Often but never always.

Melita felt uneasy, and it was over this plate of bacon and eggs that she decided to look for another place to live. Frank had been a gentleman to her, and the day he stopped being one, she didn't want her name in it.

The following Saturday the three of them dressed for a dinner engagement, but when they were about to leave a silly argument erupted over who was going to drive the car. When the argument ended, Frank refused to leave for the engagement and Sheila left with Melita.

The two of them went to a private club instead, and over drinks Sheila made a confession. "I had an affair last year, and I'm not sorry about it. I'm sick of Frank. Before you came, he made me cry every morning. I felt this big." She made the familiar gesture and dropped her hand. "There was a man on my job— married—and every morning he would compliment me. On my hair, maybe my dress, the way I smelled so nice. He was interested in my work, and we worked late one evening. Afterwards we went for a drink, and one thing led to another. We ended up at a hotel. He asked me if I loved my husband, and I couldn't even answer him."

As inexperienced as Melita was, she understood the man had been a trap. He was someone who had sensed unhappiness and neglect and found an opportunity. And couldn't Sheila do better than a married man? Married men were the worst kind of baggage, full of unrecognized guilt and too many obligations. "What did you do after this? Did you still work with him?"

"Yes. I saw him for a whole year."

"How did it end?"

"He was transferred, and I got a job teaching, which is what I really wanted to do. It all happened after Frank told me about the baby."

Melita frowned. "What baby? What are you talking about?"

"We were arguing about having children, and he said it was all right if I didn't want children because he has a child. Right here in the city. It happened my last year of college. You know he finished a year before I did, and he wanted to marry me, but I wanted to finish school. So he came back to Philly and started working."

"But he visited you a lot during your senior year."

"I know. But I guess it wasn't enough, because this is when it happened. He told me he felt lonely one evening, and he went to a club and met up with a woman he knew. I don't think he had cheating in mind. It just happened."

"How old is the baby?" Melita asked.

"He's two. Frank sees him sometimes, you know—child

support. And a boy too." Melita shook her head. "Later he told me there was never a real relationship between him and the boy's mother. It's the child he's concerned about. I met him once."

"How did you feel?" Melita asked and instantly regretted it.

"It was hard."

Melita thought about the phone calls during the year. It hadn't simply been a rough patch Sheila was going through. Her marriage was under assault by anger and hurt and disappointment and deceit. A tough crowd to battle for anyone, let alone a young married couple. Melita felt hurt for her friend, and her eyes dampened a little. She blinked.

"Do you remember when I told you about my abortion?" Sheila asked.

"I remember."

"I was fifteen years old. Frank was seventeen and he begged me to marry him. He wanted to marry me and have a family. All I could see for myself was my mother's life: a pack of babies, living in the projects and always doing without something. I wanted to go to college. I didn't tell my mother about the abortion, but Frank did, and my family took me through it. Nobody in our family—relatives included—had ever aborted a baby. It just isn't done. I felt like Frank betrayed me. We broke up for a while. Sometimes I think if I had kept the baby, things might be different now …"

"You don't know this," Melita declared. "You don't know how your life would have turned out. You were fifteen and probably scared. And God forgives us our sins and mistakes."

"But we live with the consequences, don't we?" Sheila's eyes were sad.

CHAPTER FIVE

Melita began quietly looking for a place to live. The deacon she had helped with visitation at the nursing home assisted her. He felt protective of her. When she explained her living situation, he found a church member willing to rent her a room.

The decision to move out came as a hurtful surprise to Sheila. She couldn't understand how stressful it was for Melita to live in a household with constant bickering. She felt abandoned, and the day Melita moved out, the two of them were barely speaking. Melita never told her about the breakfast incident with Frank.

She solemnly packed her clothes and loaded her luggage into the trunk of the car. Sheila drove her to the house where she would be staying and helped take the luggage inside. Melita thanked her for everything, and they walked to the car. There was no embrace, no warm goodbye. Melita stood on the sidewalk and watched her friend drive away. She felt a sudden urge to run after her but only stood watching the car grow smaller and smaller with distance until she saw nothing at all.

CHAPTER SIX

"Let me show you the rest of the house." Mrs. Brooker, her new landlady, leaned heavily on her cane as she crossed the living room floor to lead Melita upstairs. She had been recently widowed and was nervous about living alone. She kept a small watchdog named Polly, and Melita had met the dog when she and her deacon visited Mrs. Brooker. During the visit she observed Polly and knew immediately that if a thief broke in and threw her a sausage, she'd forget all about her owner.

"Your room faces the backyard," Mrs. Brooker said and opened the door to a wonderful room with a high, firm bed and a heavy wooden rocking chair. There was also a dresser and a wardrobe of wood which matched the headboard of the bed. The room felt cozy, and it was very clean.

"Was this your daughter's room?" Melita asked.

"No. I never had children. No such luck." Mrs. Brooker's face became thoughtful, and Melita felt sad for her. "The bathroom is next door. I had it remodeled." They walked down the short hallway to a sea-green bathroom flooded with sunlight. The tub was low and wide, and the toilet, sink, and fixtures were new. A skylight gave the room a bright, open appearance, which the rest of the house lacked. Melita imagined the green tub filled with cool water and fat goldfish swimming happily.

"My room is next to the linen closet." Mrs. Brooker led her to a room full of expensively crafted furniture. Three windows faced the street and were curtained by sheer fabric, which framed partially closed Venetian blinds. Laundry was piled at the foot of the bed, and newspapers and magazines littered the floor. A box filled with tissue paper and what looked like dresses sat on the corner of the dresser. Dead roses filled a crystal vase on a low table near the windows.

"I know you don't have much." Mrs. Brooker spoke again, and Melita looked at her. "Why don't we go fifty-fifty? "We'll split the gas and electricity. My bills are never very high. Do you cook?"

"Yes."

"Well, you can cook your own food. I'll make space in the refrigerator for your groceries. And listen, all I ask is that you respect the house. Do you have a boyfriend?"

"No."

"Well, if you have one, he can come see you. He can visit you downstairs in the living room. And you don't have to stay in your room all the time either. You can use the rest of the house, too."

They went downstairs, and Melita brought her luggage up to her room. She had a small collection of books which she set on the dresser top beside her lotion, face cream, and deodorant. She wore very little makeup and owned no real jewelry, so the dresser top was relatively bare.

She walked over to the bedroom window and saw three dogs huddled together and imagined what they were telling each other.

Maybe they were discussing the weather or how their dog food tasted or the ways of humans. Or maybe they were all wondering when it would be warm again. Watching the dogs Melita smiled and wondered when it would be warm again too.

Mrs. Brooker in her day had been an attractive woman with amber eyes and skin the color of creamed coffee. These bits of beauty were now marred by her tacky appearance and uncombed hair. At seventy-eight she was a lonely, frightened person with few friends and a lot of money she was convinced everyone wanted. Her husband had taken good care of her during the marriage and left a generous life insurance policy when he passed.

She made up her mind about Melita right away: She was a young woman in trouble. And if she had family, they cared nothing for her. How could anyone let a young woman live on her own in a city like Philadelphia? (Mrs. Brooker was from another time when young women could walk down Broad Street on New Year's Eve night and feel safe.) Well, whatever her circumstances, she was glad for the sound of another human voice in her home and hoped Melita would stay for a long time.

CHAPTER SEVEN

Melita slowly began building a social life for herself and became fast friends with Ruby Dean, a short, brown-skinned woman with a quick mind and strong career ambitions. Her marriage of ten years had dissolved into a separation, and she and her children now lived in a large brick house with dim lighting that gave it a dark and cozy feel.

When Melita first visited Ruby, a stray dog had moved in with the family, and pieces of dry dog food had crunched underfoot as she walked from the living room to the kitchen. Ruby apologized for the mess, but Melita thought her home welcoming and warm. It was the home of a woman who worked full-time and cared for two young children. There were no man things around. No hat on the table. No big shoes in the wrong place. No scent of aftershave in the bathroom.

Ruby's main interests at this time in life were her children and her career. And Melita suited Ruby well. She loaned her money and would go clubbing with her on short notice. Melita was also fond of Ruby's children. Ruby felt comfortable with Melita and talked with her for hours about anything and everything. And although she entered their friendship with a pragmatic eye, she eventually came to value Melita for her sincerity.

Sometimes Ruby's husband came to take the children for a weekend. If Melita happened to be visiting when he arrived, Ruby would ask her to stay. During his brief visits Melita watched his eyes soften each time he looked at his wife. "When are we getting back together?" He would ask and smile at her. He behaved as if his wife was simply angry and had run away from home for a few brief hours. Ruby wouldn't answer him when he asked this question.

"I love my freedom," she was fond of saying after he left. "We don't want the same things. When we were together, all he wanted to do was party and run with a wild crowd. Partying and drinking—that was all he wanted. We had children to raise, and there he was acting like he had no responsibilities. I don't have time for his foolishness.

"I remember one time he had a party here at our house and things really got out of hand. I was upstairs with the children trying to get them to go to sleep. I went downstairs and asked him to make his friends go home. He wouldn't listen. Do you know he locked me out on the back porch? It was winter. One of his friends heard me banging on the door and let me back in the house. I couldn't live with him any more after that. I could have caught pneumonia out there on that porch. He chose his friends over his wife and children."

Ruby often peppered their conversations with memories of a marriage gone badly. Her hurt and disappointment caused her to make scornful generalizations about Black American men, something Melita didn't like. This peculiar malice toward Black men, which afflicted some Black women, had not taken root in her. She had grown up around Black men who were providers, husbands, and fathers. They made lives for themselves and their families. Imperfect, burdened, suffering, they managed to love and protect to their best. And every day they had to earn their manhood in the face of a racism that carved into their hearts and minds how lacking and insignificant they were. They were tough and yet incredibly tender and full of grace. And on Sunday mornings they dressed in their best and went to church.

In Philadelphia Melita encountered a type of Black man that was new to her. These men wanted women to provide for them. They fathered children they didn't care about—as if the children were medals for their ability to reproduce. And yet countless women pinned hopes of stability, love, and commitment on these urban warriors. Because this is what they were, at war with God, themselves, racism, and hope. And sometimes the children of these men carried their fathers' legacies right into prisons and jails. "Don't have anything to do with them," Ruby warned her. "They're the worst of the worse."

But Black men weren't the only objects of Ruby's ill will. She disliked the growing number of Asian merchants in her neighborhood. More than once, Melita witnessed Ruby's scene-making when she thought an Asian merchant behaved rudely or talked down to her. She would put her hand on her hip, narrow her eyes, and start talking loudly and badly about the store merchandise and service. The merchant would revert to his native tongue or wave his hands at her in frustration and walk away. If Ruby wanted to press her point, she would follow behind the merchant still talking loudly and finish what she had to say.

"Ruby, I can't shop with you in these stores if you keep making scenes like this," Melita told her after one outburst. "If you don't like the merchant don't shop in the store. Why go back to a store where you're treated badly? Shopping is supposed to be pleasant."

"This is my neighborhood, and I shop where I want," Ruby said.

"That doesn't make sense. If a merchant is rude to me, I tell him he's rude, and I don't shop there anymore. I don't argue."

"I can't stand those chinks." Ruby's voice became ugly.

Melita reasoned, "They're people of color just like we are, Ruby. They've suffered too."

"Not like Black people." Ruby retorted.

"We don't have a monopoly on suffering," Melita insisted. "Some of these people were in wars and lived under terrible regimes."

"All I know is they come here and get these loans and start businesses, and the white man doesn't make this kind of money available to Black people."

"So why take it out on the Asians? They're just using the system. If I went to a foreign country and the people there were loaning money to start businesses, I'd take advantage of it too."

"Why do you have to defend everybody?" Ruby asked.

"Because at some point everybody's been treated badly."

"But only our suffering has lasted longer." Ruby said.

"No, it hasn't." .

"Well, who else has suffered longer?"

"The Jews," Melita announced like a schoolgirl at her lessons.

"God's chosen people." Ruby shook her head in defeat, and Melita laughed.

The two of them often disagreed when it came to race matters. Melita had spent a lot of time listening to her mother, a college professor, talk politics and history. Exchange students from Saudi Arabia, India, Kenya, and Ghana visited their home. In high school, when other girls dreamed of romantic love, Melita read about foreign countries and dreamed of a world beyond her hometown. As an American her views were formed freely and often optimistically. She believed the world was full of people she wanted to meet and know better. And they would like her because she was an American, and Americans were known to be a generous, freedom-loving people.

For Ruby it was not so simple. Life in America was a place of confined opportunity, especially for Black people. White people were essential to her view of the world. They loomed large as oppressors and enemies of her people. She was offended by Melita's lack of racial sophistication. Melita didn't dislike white people, and whatever hurt racism brought her she kept to herself. She seldom talked about white people or their rude arrogance that led them to think too much of themselves. Ruby was determined to change Melita's view so she would see racism at work in her life and those around her. Melita observed Ruby and listened to her and tried to understand her angst, but all she saw in racism was hurt and sin. And to her mind the whole human race was guilty of the hate that led to things like racism.

CHAPTER EIGHT

The hospital job proved to be dead-end drudgery. All day Melita was crammed into a small office with three other women, filing patient records and retrieving patient information. The only bright spot in the job was looking at the babies and talking with their mothers.

One afternoon she was asked to help in the emergency room. No one else in the office wanted to help, and as the newest hire, she was sent, even though she had never worked in an emergency room. She was taken to a desk where two clerks were busy helping patients and filling out paperwork. After a few minutes of instruction, she was left on her own to page doctors and answer the information help line.

She mispronounced the name of an egotistical doctor, and he came to the desk to personally correct her in a very rude manner. A woman whose child had swallowed bleach phoned, frantic for help, and Melita didn't know what to tell her. "Read the bottle," she yelled into the receiver. A man who had been waiting for some time came to the desk and cursed at her for the slowness of the emergency room service.

After about an hour of calls for help and irate patients, a

woman stepped behind the desk and asked how things were going. "Okay," one of the clerks responded. "If you need help getting patient numbers, Melita will help you."

"Excuse me." Melita looked up at the woman, who was very tall. "Excuse me, but I have to ask my supervisor if I can do this extra work for you."

The woman looked down at Melita with curious cold blue eyes. Her face was a pale white framed by faded brown hair. "I'm the emergency room supervisor, and I tell everyone around here what to do, including your supervisor."

"I don't think you understand." Melita spoke slowly, as if the woman was mentally deficient. "When I came to help, I was told I would answer the help line and page people. I'm having a hard time doing this because it wasn't explained to me very well. I don't think I can do any more."

"When you're asked to work in a specific area of the hospital, it's understood you'll do other things too."

"But I can barely page the doctors," Melita protested. "I don't think I can retrieve patient numbers too. I wasn't shown how."

"One of the girls will show you." The woman moved away from the desk and walked down the hall.

Melita endured two more hours at the desk until Pearl showed up. "Ready for lunch?" Pearl asked. Melita glanced at her watch. It was twelve o'clock. "What's wrong?" Pearl asked. "You look sick.

"The flu is going around now ..." Melita didn't answer Pearl and tucked her purse under her arm as she left the desk. The two of them walked back to the office.

It may have been the stress of her life compounded by the loss of her mother and the adjustment to life in a big city that caused the next unfortunate incident. Melita tried to calmly explain to the office manager what had happened in the emergency room. But instead of coherent words, every bad word she had heard since childhood came roaring back to her mind. She let loose a stream of profanity that made the other women in the office stare at her in stunned silence.

Melita had always been so calm and well-mannered. But caught up in anger, she forgot all the Bible verses she had memorized about anger and cursing. Her education, the manners her mother had taught her, the piano lessons—all flew out the window as she soared on a current of verbal filth. She called the emergency room supervisor every name she could think of and created some.

The office manager, a very proper Black woman looked at Melita with eyes that asked in horror, *Where did she learn to curse like this?* She was visibly pained to have a young Black woman capable of such anger working in her office. Something would have to be done about this.

Melita was pulled from the emergency room after her lunch and sent back to her regular duties. She felt badly about her outburst and was glad to leave at the end of the day. She awoke the next morning with a fever and painful body aches. Her doctor prescribed antibiotics and three days of rest, which meant no work for the rest of the week.

When she returned to work on Monday, Mrs. Brown, the office manager, cast a skeptical eye at the doctor's excuse and told Melita she was to attend a meeting. Assuming the meeting was for all the staff, Melita was surprised to find only herself,

Mrs. Brown, and another woman. She introduced herself as Ms. Kelly—another supervisor in this overly supervised hospital that was perpetually shorthanded.

Ms. Kelly spoke first. "Melita we've had complaints about your work, and I've called this meeting to find out what's going on. You've only been here for a short while, and I really felt when I hired you that you would work out well here."

"What complaints?" Melita asked.

"That your work is unsatisfactory," Ms. Kelly replied.

"In what way?"

Ms. Kelly turned to look at her subordinate. "Mrs. Brown?"

"The files aren't done correctly, and the girls have to go behind you to straighten things out." Mrs. Brown's face filled with disgust. "And your attitude about being placed in the ER was entirely uncalled for. Your cursing when you came back to the office—I've never heard anything so vulgar and unladylike."

"Mrs. Brown talked with me once about a misplaced file, and I'm very sorry about the cursing. It won't happen again."

"I counseled her about all the mistakes she made," Mrs. Brown insisted.

Melita defended herself. "She didn't counsel me. She showed me a file I misplaced and showed me where it belonged."

"Well, when a supervisor points out a mistake you've made, it's considered counseling." Ms. Kelly's eyes looked very cold.

"But I only made one mistake."

"We can't continue to pay you if your work is unsatisfactory," Ms. Kelly said. "I would like to know how you personally feel about your job, and I think you should be honest."

Melita sat up in her chair and looked Ms. Kelly in the eye.

"When I came to Philadelphia, I did not plan on working as a file clerk. I believe I am qualified and capable of much more challenging work. The job is boring, which could be why I made the mistakes Mrs. Brown claims I made. It does not allow me to be creative and use my intellectual abilities. I took this job because I'd rather work than collect unemployment."

Ms. Kelly was caught off guard by Melita's frankness but quickly collected herself. "I think this is from your heart and you would be happier someplace else. Do you think you can finish out the day, or would you like to leave now?"

"I will leave now."

Ms. Kelly blinked. "Are you sure you want to leave?" she asked.

"Yes. I don't feel well anyway." Melita left the two of them sitting there and returned to an office swamped with work. She collected her coat and purse and said goodbye to her coworkers.

It was terrible coming home in the middle of the day. Mrs. Brooker listened to Melita's recap of the meeting and clucked. "I never liked working with Black folks," she confessed. "Just like crabs. You know, when a crab sees another about to get out of a barrel, it pulls that crab down. That's just how Black folks are. Crabs. But don't worry. We'll help each other."

Mrs. Brooker was secretly glad for Melita's misfortune. Now she would probably stay with her for a long time.

CHAPTER NINE

A few days later Melita met with her pastor believing he might be able to help her find another job. Pastor Harris held a prominent position as pastor of one of the largest congregations in Philadelphia, and his business contacts were numerous. A referral from him might open doors for her.

He looked at Melita across the expanse of his wide handsome desk and listened to her story. "I don't think the way you left the job was wise because you may need references from them," he told her. Melita looked at her pastor's well-fed face and the extra girth around his middle. What did he remember of hard times? He appeared to bury his unhappy memories each time he sat at the dinner table. It was easy for him to talk about references from people willing to fire her for a simple mistake and cursing.

Pastor Harris felt concern for Melita, but he knew very little about her and was unwilling to involve himself too directly in her life. She looked like she could be trouble for a man of God. "I'll talk with a few people and see what I can do," he said dismissively and returned to his paperwork.

Melita thanked him and left his office, believing she had accomplished nothing. She applied for unemployment compensation. But the human resources director of the hospital informed the unemployment bureau that Melita had been fired because attempts at counseling her had failed. Melita wrote the human resources director a letter telling her she planned to take legal action if her benefits were denied. The director responded by filing for a hearing. Melita needed the benefits because her savings might not last until she found another job.

She talked with the supervisor of the claims office, a pleasant, round-faced woman. "The hospital lied about me," she explained. "I wasn't counseled at all. I went to a meeting one day and was asked if I wanted to leave or finish out the day. So I left. They didn't want me anyway."

"Get a lawyer," the supervisor advised. "Anything to do with money like this, you need a lawyer."

"But I can't afford a lawyer."

"Go to Legal Aid. They're right on Broad Street."

Melita visited Legal Aid the next day. An attractive Black attorney helped her by taking information and reassuring her she would be helped. Her agitation was visible to him, and he did his best to comfort her in a professional and courteous manner. She met with him several times, and her case was eventually given to an experienced paralegal who met her the morning of the hearing.

The two of them walked into a room to find Mrs. Brown, Ms. Kelly, a woman Melita had never met, and the human resources director. The hearing began, and it was evident the four of them had spent time coordinating their lies. They claimed she had falsified her time card, was insubordinate, and didn't come to work for three days. No mention was made of her doctor's excuse. Mrs. Brown, the only Black woman in the room, insisted she had counseled Melita. Ms. Kelly said nothing, and the woman Melita had never met looked uneasy—as if she had been forced to attend. The human resources director glared at her the whole time.

The hearing dragged on and on and became an exercise in female pettiness. Mercifully the arbitrator put a stop to it: "You'll be notified by mail once a decision is reached," she told them and left the room.

Melita went home and prayed. A week later she received a letter. The hospital had lost its case against her, and her benefits would continue. She thanked God and started looking for another job.

CHAPTER TEN

The search for work seemed futile. A few companies wrote and thanked her for her résumé and interest but had no openings that fitted her qualifications, or else they weren't hiring at all. Pastor Harris phoned on a warm spring evening and suggested career counseling. "I called an acquaintance of mine. He works as an interviewer for an employment agency. He places people in jobs with private industry. Can you meet him Wednesday at one?"

"Of course." Melita felt happy. Work at last. Pastor Harris gave her the counselor's name and the address of the agency. The day of the interview she dressed carefully and said a prayer. The office wasn't difficult to find, and the counselor introduced himself as Mr. Ormond. He was fair-skinned and a little overweight, and he wore his hair in a short afro.

Melita sat in his office filling out a preliminary form and felt his eyes on her legs. She finished the form quickly. Mr. Ormond studied the information for a few moments, looked over her résumé, and made a phone call. He talked briefly with someone and replaced the receiver. "I have something you might be interested in. There's an insurance company in Center City that has a training program. The job pays well. Would you like to talk with them?"

"Yes. What's the address?"

"I'll take you there. I know the human resources director, and he's always looking for good prospects."

On their way out of the building they passed the receptionist, and Melita saw her give Mr. Ormond a look of disapproval and wondered. The train ride to Center City gave him time to ask Melita about herself. She found his line of questioning odd for an employment counselor. "What's important to you in life?" he asked.

"What do you mean?" She turned from the window to look at him.

"What matters to you most right now?"

"Being able to support myself. Making a life for myself that I can enjoy while I'm single."

"Is there anything else?"

Melita thought a few seconds. "Having good friends is very important."

Mr. Ormond rested his hand on hers. "I would like to be your friend," he said in his most sincere voice.

Oh no, Melita thought. *I must really look naive.* She pulled her hand away and thanked him for his offer of friendship. "You're very kind," she told him.

"Have you had lunch?"

"No." Her stomach knotted slightly.

"I'd like to take you to lunch."

"That's all right. I'm not very hungry."

"Please. I'd like to," he insisted. "Only if it's no trouble."

Melita decided it wasn't. But as they ate lunch at a cafeteria, she had the uneasy feeling that things had taken a wrong turn. She picked at her lunch and swallowed a few mouthfuls of food. Mr. Ormond seemed very relaxed and displayed the confidence of a cat playing with a mouse it intended to eat.

They arrived at the insurance company and waited in the elegant lobby for close to twenty minutes. The director was not in, which seemed strange to her because Mr. Ormond had phoned to let him know they were coming. She looked down at her aching feet. "I think we should reschedule this," she suggested.

He shrugged. "That's fine with me. I'll walk you to the train." As they approached the depot he asked what her plans were for the rest of the day.

"I don't have any immediate plans."

"It's such a lovely day. Why don't we go to the park?"

"Don't you have to get back to work?"

"No. I have days when I'm out of the office on business."

Melita resisted. "I'm not wearing shoes for the park."

"I'll buy you a pair," he offered.

"No."

"Come on," he insisted. She hesitated and then wondered what harm there could be in going to a public park with him. After all he had been recommended by Pastor Harris. He wouldn't set her up with a rapist or murderer. "I don't get to do nice things for a woman like you," he gently explained. "Please give me this chance." He sounded sad and kind of lonely to Melita.

"Okay. I'll go to the park but only for a little while." It might be nice to walk and talk. He handed her a twenty-dollar bill and disappeared into a nearby store. Melita thought about tucking

43

the money in her purse and leaving. Instead, she bought a pair of low-heeled sandals and gave him his change when he reappeared.

"Most women wouldn't have returned the change," he said.

"I'm not most women," she replied.

Once they were seated on the train, he told her he had to go home and change his clothes. "Change your clothes? For what?"

"It won't take long." They rode the rest of the way in silence. Melita wasn't sure what to do now. This whole experience was new to her.

"I'll wait outside," she told him after they walked the three blocks from the train to his apartment.

"Come on in. I'm not going to hurt you. I have a daughter to think about."

The apartment was spacious and orderly. Melita sat on the edge of a kitchen chair near the door and waited while he changed his clothes. He came into the kitchen dressed in jeans, tennis shoes, and a short-sleeved shirt. Then he opened his briefcase and took out a bottle of vodka. He had gone into a liquor store after giving her the twenty-dollar bill. "I thought we were going to the park," she reminded him thinking of how badly she needed a job.

"We are."

"So, why are you pouring yourself a drink?"

"Just be patient. Want some?" He held the bottle out to her.

"No."

"A real Christian." He toasted her. They sat at the table looking at each other. "Please have some. I won't get you drunk."

"You can't get me drunk," she told him and stood up, opened a cupboard, and chose a glass. She poured enough vodka to cover the bottom of the glass and filled the rest with orange juice.

Mr. Ormond finished his drink and began pouring out his troubles to her. He couldn't find a decent woman. He was divorced and looking for a good woman to settle down with him. He told Melita all about his sorry ex-wife and how much money he made. "You could marry me." He poured himself another drink. "I'm twenty-eight years old and I have a good job. I can give anything you want. You don't seem greedy. I know I could satisfy you."

"In what way?" Melita crossed her legs and leaned forward listening intently for his answer.

"Materially. Sexually."

"I don't even know you. How can I marry you?" she asked.

"I'm telling you about me."

"You don't get to know a person over a drink and an exchange of information—and what about love?"

"Love. That's all you women think about."

"Because love is real. It's not full of lies and games. And instead of sitting here telling me your troubles, we could be walking in the park."

"Okay. Let's go." He sighed. 'Wait. I want to get my backgammon set and a blanket."

The park wasn't far, and it was beautiful with lush green trees and acres of well-kept grass and flowers. Melita felt a pang of homesickness remembering how carefully her father had cared for the lawn and flowers of their home. He seemed to love every blade of grass, and she remembered watching him water the lawn on summer days—totally relaxed and at ease with God's creation.

Halfway through a game of badly played backgammon, Melita asked about rescheduling her appointment with the insurance company. Mr. Ormond looked at her. "You blew it." His voice became ugly and cold. 'You have to play by my rules." Melita knew what he meant and stood up clutching her purse.

"I didn't ask to see you," she explained. "I didn't ask for your help. I was referred to you. You seem lonely—begging a stranger to spend time with you. If you had other motives, that's your problem. I'll mail you a check for the shoes." She began walking away.

"Go tell your pastor," he yelled. "See what he says. Why do you think he sent you to me?"

Melita had no idea how to get home and kept walking. After a while a young white boy appeared out of nowhere. He came down the street pushing a bicycle. He must have been about twelve or thirteen years old. She wondered why he wasn't in school. He looked friendly enough as he came closer. Melita didn't know if he would speak to a stranger but took a chance and asked for directions. The boy politely gave her the name of the bus she should take and walked her to the bus stop. "Is this a dangerous neighborhood?" she asked.

"No. It's safe. Just stay on the street. The bus should be here in about ten minutes."

Melita looked at the freckles splashed across his face. "Thank you," she said. He walked on, pushing his bike. He had been so relaxed and friendly as he helped her. She didn't want him to go. He made her feel safe, if only for a moment. Melita felt badly about going to Mr. Ormond's apartment. What would she tell Pastor Harris if he asked about the interview?

CHAPTER ELEVEN

"You need to tell Pastor Harris." Ruby angrily slammed the refrigerator door and set two sodas on the table.

"I'm too ashamed." Melita watched her pour the sodas into two glasses. "I did go to his apartment."

"But you didn't do anything. I'd tell Pastor about him."

"He called me the next day to tell me he could set up another interview with the human resources director."

"That's the least he could do. You're supposed to have sex with him for a pair of shoes and the promise of an interview. He didn't apologize either, did he?"

"No."

"You know, if he was sincere, he could have called you and blamed it on the liquor just to save face and see you again."

"I don't want to see him again." Melita's voice rose, and Ruby saw the distress in her eyes. "I've never been propositioned about a job before. Not ever by anyone. Do you know what's strange?"

"What?"

"When we reached the insurance company, the person we were supposed to meet wasn't even there. And before we left the office, Mr. Ormond called to let him know we were coming."

"How do you know he called?" Ruby asked.

"I was right there."

"He probably called time and temperature and talked to the recording. The whole thing sounds like a setup to me. He planned that whole mess to get you to his apartment. I know these men."

"I didn't think of it as a setup," Melita explained. "I was too busy trying to stay one step ahead of him and get a job."

"I'd tell Pastor Harris," Ruby urged. "I would."

"What good would it do?"

"What good would it do? Well, for one thing he could stop sending women to this man. You don't know how many women he's treated like this." Melita finished her soda and became quiet. Ruby rinsed the glasses and set them in the sink for later washing. "Why don't you stay for dinner? The children will be glad to see you. They're upstairs." She took plastic containers out of the refrigerator. "Nothing special—just leftovers."

Melita decided to tell Pastor Harris about the botched meeting with Mr. Ormond. "I was surprised to learn Richard behaved like this," he told her. Melita looked at him across the wide expanse of his handsome desk. He suddenly looked like a man who couldn't be trusted. "I thought of talking to him, but I don't believe this is necessary. I know I won't be sending any more women to him."

His words sounded hollow and insincere. Melita looked into his eyes and believed he knew what kind of man he had sent her to see. A nasty male plot had been planned at her expense. Mr. Ormond's words echoed in her mind: *Why do you think he sent you to me?*

She spent the rest of the spring looking for work, attending church, and dancing at what must have been the last disco in

Philadelphia. The Christians she befriended at this time were worldly people. Carnal. They spent time in bars and lounges. Some of them had illicit sexual affairs and talked badly about one another. They were all competitive and materialistic—people out for the so-called good life. Melita became comfortable with them and questioned what she had been taught about the Christian way of life. From all appearances they seemed to be doing all right as they went about their lives and treated the church like a big club ...

CHAPTER TWELVE

Spring eased into summer, and life with Mrs. Brooker became routine. Melita managed to listen to her boring stories about her past life with a straight face. She never saw Mrs. Brooker with a book in her hands, not even a Bible. She read the *Philadelphia Inquirer*, smearing it with whatever she had eaten for breakfast, and watched a lot of television or sat on her enclosed porch and looked at the people passing.

Melita did the household chores and helped Mrs. Brooker with grocery shopping. She offered to do the cooking, but Mrs. Brooker jealously guarded the little independence she had and refused Melita's help in the kitchen. She spilled food on the kitchen floor and the table where it dried until Melita wiped it away. She stored dirty pots with clean ones, and the kitchen became a harbor for roaches. But she blamed the roaches on her next-door neighbor, the woman with the dogs. She claimed the roaches were attracted to dog food. Melita cooked her own food and prayed Mrs. Brooker wouldn't start a fire in the kitchen.

One Sunday morning Melita dressed for church and had an uneasy feeling about leaving her alone. She had dragged herself around all Saturday and was very quiet that morning. Melita undressed and put on her jeans and a T-shirt. "Melita! Melita!" Mrs. Brooker's voice sounded brittle and on edge.

Melita opened her bedroom door. "Yes?"

"Come here." Melita walked down the hall and found her in the bathroom staring at the tub. "Rinse that out!" she snapped.

"What?"

"That!" Melita looked at the tub. There was no ring and no scum. Then she saw it—a thin residue of cleanser she had not rinsed entirely away after scrubbing. She rinsed the tub, and Mrs. Brooker watched for a second or two and walked back into her bedroom.

Melita came out of the bathroom and saw her sitting in a chair fanning herself. "What's wrong?" she asked.

"I'm sick." Mrs. Brooker slumped forward, still attempting to fan herself.

"Do you want me to get you something?"

"No, I'll be all right." Melita went downstairs for a cup of tea. A little later Mrs. Brooker came down the stairs, holding on to the rail to steady herself.

"Maybe you should lie down," Melita suggested.

"I'm going to get some orange juice and see if I don't feel better."

Melita left the room to sit on the porch and sip her tea. "Melita!" She went back into the kitchen. Mrs. Brooker sat at the table holding on to its sides. "Give me that bucket on the back porch."

Melita brought the bucket, and Mrs. Brooker vomited into it. "I think you should go to the hospital," she urged.

"I don't want to go to the hospital."

"I think you should. I can call someone to take you there."

"No."

Well, die then, Melita thought and went back upstairs. The kitchen phone rang, and somehow Mrs. Brooker managed to answer it.

Minutes later the doorbell rang. Melita went back downstairs to answer the door. It was the cross-eyed neighbor from down the street. She rushed past Melita into the living room. "She's in the kitchen." Melita told her.

The neighbor took one look at her friend. "Come on, Eva. We're going to the hospital." Then she gave Melita a menacing look. "You should have called me."

"She didn't want me to call anyone, and I'm not a nurse. All I could do was offer to help her."

"You still should have called me."

"I don't even know your number."

"Eva would have given it to you."

"She didn't want to give me any numbers." Melita's voice rose and she felt defensive.

The neighbor called an ambulance and began getting Mrs. Brooker ready to leave. The ambulance came within fifteen minutes. But it seemed like an eternity with the cross-eyed neighbor glaring at her with her good eye and Mrs. Brooker slumped over in a chair.

She had suffered a mild heart attack and stayed in the hospital for a week. Melita took care of the house and faithfully fed and walked the dog. The neighbor came every day to make sure the dog had been walked. But Melita knew she had really come to check on her and take reports back to Mrs. Brooker.

When Mrs. Brooker came home from the hospital, Pastor Harris asked Melita if she could come by his office sometime. He wanted to talk with her. Curious as to what he might want, Melita met with him.

They sat in his office squarely facing each other. "How are you and Mrs. Brooker getting along?" he asked.

"One time she told me I'm a hard person to live with." Melita revealed.

"Do you think she's right?"

"Maybe. But she's not the easiest person to live with either."

"She's older and set in her ways." He looked thoughtful for a moment. "I'm concerned because I don't think she's very happy with the way things are working out."

Naturally he was concerned for Mrs. Brooker. Her husband had been a church trustee and given generously of his time and money. Melita was a nobody without a job and no family around to care for her. "Mrs. Brooker has been lonely since her husband died, and she was looking for someone she could adopt for company."

"My mother died a year ago and no one can take her place," Melita said evenly.

"I don't think Mrs. Brooker could be a mother to you, but I was thinking you could spend more time with her. Be more attentive. Buy her a plant, or play board games with her."

"I've thought about combing her hair," Melita offered. Mrs. Brooker's hair always looked a mess between visits to her hairdresser.

Pastor Harris raised his eyebrows. "I don't know about

combing her hair ... maybe you could find some ways to help her occupy her time."

"I understand what you're saying, but I have my own plans."

"I'm not saying stay there if you have someplace else to go. Do you have someplace else?" Melita looked down, and the full brunt of her situation hit her. She was alone in a big city with no family and at the present time no job. All she had was a crusty old woman with a dog and a rented room in her house and a fat pastor who didn't seem to care about her.

"I'll try to be nicer." She said and left his office feeling defeated. And for a whole month Melita tried. She spent more time at home. She read the Bible to Mrs. Brooker and watched television with her. When she had errands to run, Melita accompanied her. But her efforts came to nothing. Mrs. Brooker changed the locks on her doors and didn't give Melita a key. It was bizarre behavior. Mrs. Brooker now seemed to believe she could not be trusted. It was embarrassing to stand on the street waiting to be let into the house.

As her living situation deteriorated, Pastor Harris offered her a job as a file clerk in his office. It seemed he had forgotten the mess she made of her job as a hospital file clerk. And did the church even need a file clerk? They had a secretary. Her unemployment compensation had run out, so she accepted.

The first time Pastor Harris asked her to get coffee for him she stared at him. "Can't you get your own coffee?" she asked.

"Miss Logan, I am paying you to help me, and making me coffee is part of your job."

Melita made the coffee. He even had her dialing numbers for him and then handing the receiver to him. Melita thought it was disgraceful for a man of his standing to behave this way.

"I'm not ungrateful," she explained to Ruby when they talked. "But he has a lot of influence in this city. Or at least he acts like he does. He has my résumé in his files, and the best he can come up with is church file clerk. I have a degree."

"But think of your work history. You haven't had much work experience."

"I wouldn't have a problem doing factory work again."

"Maybe he's still looking for something for you. He's the only Black man in Philadelphia worth anything as far as I'm concerned. And he's helped a lot of people in this town." Ruby refused to speak badly about him. Melita didn't share with Ruby the uneasiness she felt about working for him.

She was relieved when he left his office to visit the sick or attend a meeting somewhere. She organized his books, made sure his desk was in order, put paper in the copier, wiped down the telephone and receiver, made the coffee, and dusted the office.

Aside from this there was never much work, and she spent most of her time talking with the church secretary, who told her, "He's just doing this to help you." She was another Pastor Harris admirer.

But Melita did eventually find work in a hospital and smiled happily as she handed Pastor Harris a letter of resignation. "Well, Miss Logan, it looks like you're going to make it anyhow." He looked over the letter and up at her. She stood in front of his desk looking down at him and inwardly rejoicing. No more coffee making. No more filing. No more dusting. No books to arrange and rearrange. No more afternoons repairing damaged hymnals. No more sitting alone in the sanctuary at times and wondering if God still loved her.

CHAPTER THIRTEEN

The new job required a few weeks of classes and on-the-job training. Once the training was completed, she would care for asthmatics, patients with chronic lung diseases, and patients recovering from open-heart surgery. It wasn't complicated work, and with a survivor's instinct Melita mastered the classes and learned the job well.

She quickly became a welcome sight to patients who appreciated her compassion and gentleness. They learned she was a sympathetic listener and sometimes told her their troubles. They took out their purses and wallets and showed her pictures of family members and even their pets. Melita found herself quickly eating lunch during her break so she could spend time with patients who seemed lonely or sad.

For Melita the hardest part of her work was watching the approach of death. In the first few months she met a young girl who seemed happy to see her each day. She was dying of leukemia and needed oxygen to ease her breathing. A part of Melita's job involved checking oxygen equipment in her room. The evening of her death it hurt Melita to find the young girl's brother and mother at her bedside listening as she made her final goodbye. She gasped for breath and spoke of her love for them and how much they had meant to her.

Melita watched this scene of sorrow and relinquishment and left the room with tears brimming. She found an exit door that led to a stairwell and sat weeping and remembering what she too had lost. Death was unfair, taking joy and laughter and most of all the presence of love inside another human being.

But death became easier to face as time passed. Melita saw shadows pass through the hallways of the hospital on sunny days and wasn't afraid. She believed it was only angels coming to claim for God what had always belonged to Him.

CHAPTER FOURTEEN

Melita saved her money and looked for an apartment taking Ruby along to serve as a second pair of eyes. She settled on a one-bedroom in Germantown. The building was old but secure with the manager and his wife living on the premises.

When she told Mrs. Brooker she was moving out, Mrs. Brooker demanded money from her. "For what?" Melita asked, puzzled.

Mrs. Brooker blinked. "I didn't take a security deposit from you."

"You never asked for one."

"Yes, I did. It's always like this when you rent a room." Mrs. Brooker blinked again. "You owe me one hundred dollars."

"But you didn't ask for a deposit when I moved in," Melita reminded her. "You said we would split the gas and electric bills, and remember, when I got my job at the hospital, I started paying for the room, and this covered everything."

"That's something you decided to do. I never agreed to it."

"You took the money, and you didn't tell me differently," Melita shot back.

"Well, all I know is you're not leaving here until I get my

hundred dollars. And if you try to leave without paying me, I'll call the police."

Now Melita had heard about Philadelphia police and read in the newspaper about some of their activities. They impressed her as officers who liked to beat on and shoot people—especially if those people were Black. An acquaintance once told her that no Black person could be arrested and taken into custody in Philadelphia without being beaten. She made it sound like an arresting requirement. Melita was afraid of them, and the last thing she wanted was to meet and greet one under bad circumstances.

She talked with Katherine, the neighbor next door who owned the dogs. "Why don't you put your things in my house?" she suggested. "I've lived next door to Eva for a long time, and she can be mean. She poisoned one of my dogs a few years ago. She might say you can't take your things out unless you pay her. It's the law, you know." Melita didn't know.

When Mrs. Brooker left to go shopping at week's end, Melita put most of her things in Katherine's house. Monday evening she came home from work to find Mrs. Brooker in a temper. "Where's your clothes?" she demanded.

"What …?"

"Where are your clothes? I want to know where your clothes are."

"I left them with a friend." Melita began to feel angry and violated.

"You were going to sneak out of this house without paying me my money," Mrs. Brooker accused.

"I wasn't going to sneak out, and I don't owe you any money."

Mrs. Brooker followed her upstairs and into her room, where

Melita put down her purse and began packing the rest of her belongings in a box. "You're not taking another thing out of this house until I get my money," Mrs. Brooker hissed. "I opened my home to you."

"I don't owe you anything." Melita threw things into the box. "I cleaned for you. I took care of your dog when you were sick. I respected your home, and I know you called Katherine to check on me while you were in the hospital. She told me you called her every night, asking if there was any traffic going in and out of your house. If I didn't bring men here while you were at home, I didn't bring them while you were away. I did you a favor living with you. A lot of old people would be glad to have me in their home."

Mrs. Brooker clenched her fist and took a step toward Melita. "Don't you dare come near me." Melita's voice became low and threatening. She had never hit an elder, but if Mrs. Brooker tried to lay a hand on her she was ready to fight. Mrs. Brooker stepped back, surprised.

"I always had the feeling you looked through my things. I don't even have privacy here. And you talked badly about me to your cross-eyed neighbor up the street. I could tell by the way she looked at me in church—all those dirty looks. Some Christian you are." Melita closed the box.

"I want to know where the rest of your clothes are," Mrs. Brooker insisted.

"My clothes are at Katherine's—next door." Melita's indignation mounted.

The phone rang downstairs, and Mrs. Brooker went to answer it. Melita hoped it might be Deacon Bale. She had talked with him about her situation and the money Mrs. Brooker demanded. And so far, neither her deacon or Pastor Harris had intervened to help her or to reason with Mrs. Brooker.

After a few minutes Mrs. Brooker came back upstairs and walked into the room. "Get out of here," Melita shouted. "I paid for this room." And she tried to take the box out of the room, but Mrs. Brooker blocked the doorway with her body. They were very near the top of the stairs, and for one horrible moment Melita wanted to give her a mighty shove down those stairs. But she quickly recovered herself. A fall downstairs could kill Mrs. Brooker and turn Melita into a murderer.

She put the box down and wrote Mrs. Brooker a check for one hundred dollars and gave it to her.

Ruby came, and together they loaded the luggage and clothes she had stored at Katherine's into Ruby's car. Melita retrieved her box and walked out of the house without saying goodbye. Mrs. Brooker stood in the doorway of her home clenching her fists and watching the car drive away. She died a few months later.

CHAPTER FIFTEEN

The year 1980 saw a creeping polarization taking place in America. The Democratic party was becoming the party of liberals and minorities—a code word for Black Americans. The Republican party, forgetting its anti-slavery roots, was presented as the party of predominately white and conservative people. Or at least this was the way the media portrayed the two parties.

And there was a lot of noise about the Moral Majority that was difficult to figure out. Who were these moral people? Abortion on demand, pornography, child abuse, rampant divorce, homosexuality, lesbianism, substance abuse, poverty, and homelessness were commonplace. People had to be doing these things in great numbers for it to even get public notice. It all puzzled Melita.

But it didn't alienate her. She had grown up helping her mother, a politically active woman, with local and national campaigns. The two of them visited neighbors and Melita listened as the adults discussed political and social issues. Her mother encouraged their community to vote, and their home became a beehive of campaign workers typing, talking, and planning. It may have been these memories that prompted Melita to help a local candidate who was campaigning for senator.

The whole city of Philadelphia had become a flurry of activity as it set in motion its huge political machinery that year. In September Melita watched a small copy shop transform into campaign headquarters for its owner. It was a small, clean place, and upon entering she was the only customer. A young woman stacked papers in trays on the counter. "Do you put together résumés?" Melita asked.

"No. We only do copies," The young lady told her. "We can copy it for you if it's already typed the way you want it. I can do a sample for you."

Melita handed her a résumé just as Raymond Davis, the owner, walked out from the back of the shop. He approached the counter and stood looking at Melita. "Would you like to work in my campaign?" he asked.

The young woman handed Melita a sample of her résumé, and she looked at it, not answering him. "I need three copies," she said and then looked up at Raymond, who was staring at her intently. "Did you ask me something?"

"Yes. I asked if you would like to work in my campaign."

"Oh, you're the one campaigning. I have thought about helping in the campaign, but I don't know what you're running for or against."

"I'm running for state senator, and I'm a Republican." He waited a moment to see what impact this would have on her.

Melita made a face at him. The only Black Republican she had known was a funeral director in her hometown. Her mother spoke of him as if he had a rare disease. "Why the face?" Raymond asked.

"I'm a Democrat."

"So?"

"I'm not thinking of changing."

"You don't have to change parties to work with me. Just vote on the issues—taxes, military spending, social programs, education. A lot of people will be doing this come November fourth. I think Black people should cover all the bases and stop throwing so much support behind the Democrats. Democrats take the Black vote for granted anyway. Did you know that before Franklin Roosevelt's administration most Black Americans were Republicans? We were the last group to go over to Roosevelt." Raymond had stuffed his hands into his pants pockets and leaned forward as if addressing an audience.

"What's your name?" Melita asked.

"I'm sorry. My name is Raymond Davis." He took two tickets from a stack on a shelf behind the counter. "If you're not busy come to this. It's a promotional kind of thing. I'd like you to come and bring a friend."

He pressed the tickets into her hand. This small request touched a need in her to feel welcomed and made a part of something much larger than herself.

"I'd really like you to be a part of my campaign, but you haven't told me your name."

"Melita. Melita Logan."

"I'll see you there?" he asked.

"Maybe," she calmly replied. But Raymond saw the brightness in her dark eyes.

Raymond Davis had a killer smile, nine hundred thousand dollars in the bank and a sexual charisma that had been the undoing of many a woman far wiser and experienced than Melita. In the thirty-fifth year of his life, he felt the winds of change blowing and wanted to cash in on the coming Republican Revolution. He believed this revolution would lift Black Americans into the ranks of the middle class in numbers never seen before and perhaps give the party a new appeal.

To make himself highly visible Raymond set up his campaign headquarters in the heart of the district he hoped to win. He learned all the Republican campaign slogans, shook numerous hands at numerous events and appeared to be a man of great understanding, intelligence, and empathy. But he lacked the common touch, that man-of-the-people charm that tended to attract the kind of people who composed a significant portion of the district. He came across as an elitist. One whose education, manners, and carriage set him too much apart from those he wanted to represent.

His opponent, John Etheridge was just as wealthy and well educated but voters could imagine John Etheridge relaxed and at ease at a family reunion with a plate of barbecue and potato salad. The fact that he was white was not a hindrance because Black voters had been voting white for generations. But Raymond Davis? He was a Republican, and his being Black didn't matter. He was still a Republican. And there was something about his wingtip shoes that didn't sit well with some constituents.

Melita took Ruby to meet him, and she was not impressed. "A Black Republican?" she asked as they left the shop.

"You should talk to him sometime and let him explain why. I

have tickets to an event he's giving. I think it's some kind of rally. We could go and—"

"No," Ruby said. "I'm too busy." Ruby was going through divorce proceedings and struggling with the emotional wreckage of her married life.

"You sure?" Melita asked.

"Yes. And Melita, don't look for anything from him."

"Why would you say that?"

"Just don't. You'll be hurt, okay?"

"You know what? I think you're sad about the divorce. But don't worry about me. I don't want anything from him. It's just something to do."

At the event Raymond watched Melita as she talked with some supporters and humored others. He came over to her several times and asked whether she wanted anything and what she thought of the gathering. "Maybe you'll be able to volunteer some time after all," he suggested.

"Maybe."

"What kind of work do you do?"

"I work at a hospital. Patient care."

"Do you like it?" he asked.

"It's a living."

"Sometimes people get jobs through the campaign—especially when their candidate wins. I'll talk with you about it later. I have to go back to a few people." He left her side, and Melita turned to talk with a woman standing beside her.

The evening ended in a shower of confetti, balloons, and streamers, and Melita laughed at the sight of Raymond standing in the middle of the floor with confetti in his hair and on his shoulders. He looked at Melita through the falling confetti and winked.

He insisted on taking her home, and during most of the ride he was quiet and thoughtful. They drove along rain-wet streets, and the city lights became colorful streamers reflected in the car windows. 'I'm glad you could make it but why didn't you bring a friend?" he asked when he stopped in front of her apartment building.

"She couldn't come."

"Not even a boyfriend?" he persisted.

"No. No boyfriend."

"That's hard to believe." He got out of the car and walked around to open the door for her. 'Saturday evening we're having a meeting at my home to plan a few things. Come if you can." He walked her to the entrance and saw her safely inside. Melita listened to his car drive away and felt an awful loneliness wash over her. She decided to throw herself wholeheartedly into his campaign.

CHAPTER SIXTEEN

Raymond's home was a sturdy brick row house he kept clean and orderly. Melita thought it strange that she hadn't considered whether he was married or single, but apparently he lived alone. She met and talked with his campaign workers—many of them women. The meetings were held regularly, and as the campaign progressed, Melita found herself totally absorbed. It was like visiting a part of her life that she had shared with her mother.

Raymond took note of her enthusiasm. "You really like this don't you?" he commented. "I think you're a natural."

"I used to help my mom when she worked on campaigns." Melita stapled flyers together and stacked them neatly on his dining room table.

"Have you thought about accepting a job with me if I win?"

"I don't think I could accept a job. Would I have to leave Philadelphia?"

"No. You could stay here and work out of my office here. Just think about it. You're a natural."

A cool autumn evening found the two of them working together after the other workers had left and gone home. Melita sat at the dining room table that was littered with paper, pencils, pens, a map, and index cards. Raymond paced restlessly up and down the floor dictating the rough draft of a speech and answering the phone at intervals. Melita, busy writing, looked up to find him staring at her. 'How about some tea?" he asked and went into the kitchen.

Melita stood up to stretch her legs. She walked into the kitchen and up to the stove where Raymond was placing the tea kettle. He turned and kissed her. His arms closed around her body in one engulfing embrace. Melita smelled the faint scent of soap on his skin and felt the softness of his flannel shirt beneath her hands. His kisses were warm and gentle. Her mind cleared enough for her to think of fleeing, and as if reading her thoughts, Raymond kissed her again and again. And afterward she didn't want to go home. She didn't want to go back to the aloneness of her tender life—that scrubbed apartment and no one to talk with. When Raymond held her, the warmth of his body, the closeness of him, seemed to fill every empty space in her heart. But she did go home, and that night after showering, she lay down still thinking of him and dreaming of being loved and at home again.

In a long-ago world, Raymond would have loved Melita. This is how it had once been between men and women. Melita would have become his the moment he opened her body with himself. Their combination of passion, intelligence, and chemistry would have held them together long enough for love to grow and bind them to one another. Raymond understood this. He knew he should keep her. It had happened this fast for him once before, and he had let the woman go. But Melita was different. He knew he could love her in the deepest of ways. But this kind of love would complicate his life and divide his attention. He would enjoy her while he had her and make love to her with every chance that came his way. And the relationship would go no further.

Melita, for her part, felt ashamed and guilty about their uninhibited lovemaking. She was still her mother's daughter, and Mrs. Logan had put a premium on virginity—something her slave ancestors had never been able to own. But she couldn't resist Raymond's desire for her. He was the first man to initiate her into the world of lovemaking. He wasn't a fumbling young man discovering the female body for the first time. He was worldly and sophisticated. He knew things. He had money and ambition. He was handsome, magnetic. And he wanted her. He insisted she be present at all his speaking engagements. "How did I sound?" he would ask on their way back to campaign headquarters. "Do I need to change anything?" It was flattering.

Raymond gave her no gifts or money, none of the nice things experienced women demanded of their lovers. The novelty of it all and the desires it awakened in her overshadowed any demands she would have made if she had known how. In her naivete being wanted and desired and having the warmth of a man in her life were enough.

CHAPTER SEVENTEEN

Melita was surprised to see a new campaign worker behind the copy desk one evening. She had dropped off some papers to be printed as flyers and introduced herself. "I'm Brenda. Raymond's told me so much about you." Melita smiled weakly. The woman was tall, big-breasted, a little on the heavy side, and white. Not pretty—just average-looking with shoulder length brown hair.

"Where's Raymond?" Melita asked.

"He had a campaign speech to make, but he told me you'd be by."

"When did you start working here?" Melita asked. "I was working as a waitress a few weeks ago and Raymond offered me a job here. But I only work evenings. I'm in school right now." The two of them engaged in small talk for a few moments, and Melita left feeling strangely betrayed.

"I met her in at a subway stop, and we talked," Raymond explained later. They sat at a table in a small coffee shop. Melita watched his fingers nervously tapping on the tabletop. "She needed a different job because she's in school, and I told her she could work part-time for me. It's nothing. I'm taking you to Harrisburg."

In that moment Melita's gut impulse was to cut Raymond and his campaign loose. But she ignored it. She continued to coordinate campaign activities, critiqued his speeches, and wrote letters and reminders. Brenda became a minor distraction.

Near the close of campaigning, she spent a day off helping workers in west Philadelphia. Raymond had planned to meet her there, but when he didn't show, she stopped by the shop expecting to find him there. She had been inside for a few minutes blowing on her hands to warm them and talking with Brenda when Raymond walked in. At the sight of him, Brenda's face lit up. Raymond spoke casually to Melita and began talking with Brenda. Melita looked at the two of them and felt herself being swept aside like so much lint. The intuition that there was more than work between Raymond and Brenda jarred her. She resisted the impulse to strike him and hurt him and instead turned around and hurried out of the door, hoping to hide herself in the crowds on Chelten Avenue. The people on the avenue didn't know her. They wouldn't see her humiliation and embarrassment, her pain.

Someone called to her. If she walked very fast, she would be in her apartment away from that voice. She could close the door on this terrible mistake she had made—giving herself away. Her mother must never know about this because for one mad moment it seemed her mother was still alive.

She heard someone calling her name. How did Raymond get in front of her on this crowded street? "I only have one thing on my mind, and it's winning. Outside of this I don't have any other considerations." His voice sounded distant. Blurred. But she could see him now. She had been blinded. Blinded by what he appeared to be. All his appeal had only been window dressing for a shabby interior. He was full of selfishness. He used people. He was unkind.

She hurried past him, almost shuddering, and reached Wayne Avenue where she leaned against a small tree feeling weak and drained. An elderly Black man looked at her with wondering eyes and approached. "Are you all right?" he asked.

"Yes." Her voice sounded thin and broken.

"Are you sure?" Melita looked at the man and said nothing. He waited with an almost fatherly concern.

"I'll be all right. Thank you." He walked away, and she continued her forever walk home.

CHAPTER EIGHTEEN

She managed to open the door to her apartment and dropped her purse on the floor. Her hands trembled, and she pressed them to her chest. There was no one at home. No one to run to with this new hurt. She sobbed a great heaving sob. A sob that ushered in tears and the sound of her young voice wordlessly releasing disappointment and pain.

She walked to her bedroom and lay across the bed without removing her coat. The evening streetlight behind a tree cast dark leaves on her bedroom wall. Silent witnesses to her tears. When she stopped crying, she watched the leaves dance and sway on the wall, thinking quietly of what had happened to her and wondering: Why did people behave as if sex was such a casual thing like combing your hair or pulling on a pair of socks? Why did people act like it was possible to have sex with someone and forget about it later? Forget the person, the words spoken, the time, the place, and the emotions?

It was all lies. Sex had to be the most binding and searing of acts to touch anyone's life. It had been this way for her, and she couldn't imagine ever feeling differently. Maybe her mother had understood this about her. Maybe her mother had tried to protect her with old-fashioned views about virginity. Maybe. She watched the leaves until a deep weariness washed over her and welcomed sleep.

The phone rang loudly and insistently. Melita stirred and opened her eyes. It was morning. She was still in her coat. She felt along the floor for the phone. "I need you to go to west Philadelphia." It was Raymond. No hesitation. No explanation. No excuse. No "Are you okay? Did I do something to upset you?" Nothing. "Are you there?" he asked.

"I work today. I have a three to eleven shift."

"Not today. Two days from now. Can you do it?"

The nerve of him. "No." She hung up the phone and quit the campaign.

Raymond lost the senatorial election by thirty thousand votes, and a week later there was a terrible fire at his home. Melita heard about the fire at work while listening to the radio in the staff room. Her heart filled with an unholy glee. Fire had touched his life. He had been paid back. Too bad he wasn't burned up with the house.

But days into December she couldn't walk past the darkened copy shop without feeling sad. One evening she saw a light dimly shining and looked in to see Raymond at the counter reading a newspaper alone. She entered, and he looked up at the sound of the bell over the door. His eyes brightened at the sight of her, but she said nothing and only stood looking at him. He impulsively stepped from behind the counter to be near her. "How have you been?" he asked.

"I'm okay." A heavy silence passed between the two of them. "I heard about the fire."

"I'm staying at my other house." He shrugged it off.

"Will you run again?" Melita asked.

"Probably." She said nothing, and he studied her face before reaching out to trace her lips.

"You're not wearing lipstick."

"No one is kissing me."

He smiled a little. "A few people who worked on the campaign got jobs," he offered. "Let me know if you need anything."

"I won't need anything from you." The heavy silence passed between them again.

He took her hand and held it almost tenderly. "Take care of yourself, okay?"

"I will." She left, and the bell above the door was the only witness to their silent regret.

Melita struggled getting back to her life as it had been before Raymond. Lovemaking had been frequent and impulsive, and there was the possibility of an unplanned pregnancy. "How could you do a thing like this?" Ruby asked when Melita confided her fears. "I didn't know you were that involved with him. I thought it was just campaign work—not an affair."

"That's how it started," Melita explained. "I couldn't tell you after we got involved with each other. You had all these court dates, and you were mad at men."

"So?"

"Well, you wouldn't have liked him."

"And would I have been wrong?" Melita sighed. "Are you pregnant?"

"I don't know. I'm two weeks late."

"Well, it could be nerves making you late. You have had a

shock." Ruby shook her head. "Melita, you have no family here. Your mom is dead. You don't make enough money to support a child. What were you thinking?"

"I used a contraceptive," Melita defended herself. "At least most of the time."

"That means nothing. I have a niece walking around right now, and she's proof that a contraceptive doesn't always work. And I know you don't believe in abortion. I hope you're not pregnant. I bet that Raymond is a walking heartbreak. And if you have a baby with him, you'll be dragging yourself down, and you'll have to drag him into court for days because he won't help you on his own. I know his kind. All smooth talk and empty promises."

Ruby's words gave Melita no comfort. She went home worried and anxious. Another two weeks passed and still no period. But a sharp pain awakened her one night, and her thighs felt sticky and wet. She turned on the bedside lamp and lifted the covers and began to cry softly. There on the sheet like a giant crimson flower lay blood from her empty womb.

The following days were unusually painful and bloody. She visited her gynecologist, a gentle, sympathetic man, and he gave her a thorough exam. "I'm going to run some tests. I don't think you've miscarried, but you may have contracted an STD. If you have, and it's not treated right away, it can create complications. You should have come to me sooner. Get dressed now."

The nurse helped her down from the examining table. Melita dressed and waited for Dr. Mehlman to return. He came into the room and began writing in her chart. He then looked her fully in her face and paused before speaking. "Listen, it's none of my business," he began. 'But you're still a young woman, and you have your whole life ahead of you." Melita squinted a little and stared at his round white owl-like face. "Why don't you wait until you marry to have sex?"

"It's too late." she told him.

"What do you mean it's too late?" he asked.

"I'm not a virgin anymore."

"It doesn't matter. A lot of people live celibate lives even after trying sex. When you marry, you'll have someone who's committed to you. He'll look after you."

"How do you know this?" Melita asked.

"I've been around for a while and seen a lot. All kinds of people come through here, and I've been practicing for a while. You have the word *wife* on your forehead. I'd marry you if I was younger and had more hair."

He smiled, and Melita was unsure of how to respond.

"But seriously," he continued, "if you can't wait, make the guy use a condom. Protect yourself. You may want children someday, and you don't want any complications." He continued to look into Melita's face hoping his words were sinking in. "Nobody wants to accept it, but sex without monogamy is risky business—especially for women. And you're very vulnerable. Promise me you'll think about what I've said."

"I will," Melita promised.

"Everything looks fine. No STD. Acetaminophen should continue to help with the cramping. See you in three months for your annual."

Melita discovered the best antidote for heartache was work. For eight hours of the day her mind was busy, and she wasn't grieving her losses. She ate lima beans and cornbread for days on end. The sight of those soft peppered beans beside a golden square of cornbread comforted her. The specks of pepper contrasted against the paleness of the plump beans. The salty flavoring of the smoked ham hocks boiled down to tender pieces of deep pink meat that fell away from the bone ... the meal brought back memories of her mother and childhood days at home. Days when her father's eyes were not clouded by depression and he smiled at his children. There were ducks in the backyard and a rabbit pen to house the rabbits her brothers raised. Six chickens laid eggs, and a guinea pig squealed each time the refrigerator door opened, hoping for a green treat. Did happiness have a sound? It seemed to have one then—the sound of love taken for granted.

CHAPTER NINETEEN

Work and memories of home didn't quite comfort Melita as she had hoped, and she decided to seek help. Pastor Harris had abruptly left and been replaced by a new pastor. Pastor Leon Sykes was a soft-spoken and kind man. As the associate pastor, his role to the church at large had been one of spiritual support. When Pastor Harris left, the congregation unanimously voted Reverend Sykes in as the new leader of their congregation. He believed in prayer and was not given to displays of emotional excess in his preaching or personal life. He was an observant and patient man and as associate pastor had taught the new members class and carefully guided converts as they began their new spiritual life. When Melita had joined the church the new members class had been recommended to her, and this was how she met Pastor Sykes.

His wife was kind to her—talkative, friendly, and warm. She was a pleasant brown skinned woman with soft gray eyes and auburn hair pulled back from her face. She smelled of spices and flowers.

Now in her sadness and loneliness Melita approached Reverend Sykes after a Sunday morning service. "I was wondering if I could talk with you about some problems I'm having."

"Sure you can." He smiled. "What's a good time for you?"

"I don't work Tuesday."

"I'll be in my office Tuesday morning. I have a visitation Tuesday afternoon. Can you come at about ten o'clock?" he asked.

"Yes."

"I'll see you then."

That morning Melita waited outside his office hands folded in her lap. The church secretary tried to make small talk, but Melita didn't feel like talking and was glad when Pastor Sykes walked out of his office. She quickly stood up. 'Come on in. How do you like this cold weather?"

"It's too cold."

"Well, in a few more months spring will be here and then summer, and then we can complain about the heat." He motioned Melita to one of the soft chairs in front of his desk. "What did you want to talk about?"

The quiet coziness of his office and the sincerity of his manner after months of hurt and loss released in Melita a flood of emotion. She opened her mouth to speak, and instead of words a single sob escaped her. Wordlessly she began to cry. Pastor Sykes placed a box of tissues near her, and she dabbed at her eyes. He sat calmly and patiently until she composed herself.

And then Melita spoke to him of her mother's death, her estrangement from her father, her affair with Raymond, the loss of her virginity, and her deep loneliness and hurt at life. Pastor Sykes had no harsh words for her and let her talk until she had emptied her heart. "Death is difficult, and sometimes we don't allow ourselves time to grieve," he explained. "You haven't really had enough time to grieve over the loss of your mother. You left a painful situation, and you moved to a new city where you had no family or support system. This is really very difficult to do. And especially for a young person. How old are you?"

"Twenty-four."

"You know the world is very different now compared to when I was growing up. People married at a young age and raised children and had a whole different set of responsibilities. My mother married at seventeen, and by the time she was twenty-four, she had four children and was running a household. The world is different now, but people haven't changed. We have the same need for love and acceptance. You may feel alone, and you may believe you've done something terrible by leaving your father and having sex without being married, but this doesn't change God's love for you. He still loves you, and He's concerned about you. The fact that you are sitting here talking with me shows His love for you."

"Sometimes I think God doesn't care about me anymore," Melita confessed.

"Well, that's just a lie from Satan. He takes our feelings of loneliness and our pain and tries to convince us we're not loved. But it's a lie.

"Let's look at this. I want you to think about what I'm going to say next, and there's no disrespect intended. I know you love your father, but your father is an adult—however depressed and hurt he may be. He is responsible for his own life. It's not your job at this time in your life to care for him. If anything, your father should be advising and comforting you. You're still a young person, and you still need guidance. And as far as having sex before marriage—it's almost a way of life these days. It happens all the time. It isn't God's desire or plan for any of us to have sex without the commitment of marriage. But if you do make this choice, it doesn't lessen or change God's love for you.

"But think about this: A man like Raymond—his whole life is wrapped up in worldly gain. He's after material wealth, power, and position. Your life as a Christian isn't about these things. Raymond can't love and understand someone like you. He'll have sex with you. He'll take what you give him, but he won't commit to you or your values. I see this all the time: Christian women get wrapped up with unsaved men who don't care about living a Christian life. And it's always the woman who gets hurt. God has someone for you and the key is to wait and trust him to bring the man to you."

"I don't know if I can wait. So far I haven't."

"God will teach you how to wait. He'll help you keep yourself. And He'll handle all those sexual urges and emotions if you ask Him. I know some women want to marry, but life is so different after you marry a man and start living with him. You start to find out the little things about a person—some of them not so pleasant. And all the excitement of your sex life, the enthusiasm—it doesn't stay forever. And what do you do then? There has to be something else holding you together, or you're in trouble.

"God wants to teach you about love. Agape love. It's a love that is always giving. It's a love that wants to do more. It's the kind of love God has for us, and when we marry, God wants us to learn about and express this kind of love to our husbands and wives. God has someone for you, and He's preparing that person now even as we speak."

Reverend Sykes continued talking with Melita and answering her questions, and when Melita left his office, she felt encouraged and comforted and hopeful.

CHAPTER ONE

Milo Sanchez stood six feet and four inches tall and owned the dark beauty which had fascinated Europeans of long ago. Ebony-skinned and broad-shouldered, he was the descendant of Ladinos—free Blacks who had migrated from Spain to Puerto Rico, where they lived and worked for close to two hundred years. In the late 1900s his ancestors had emigrated to America and settled in Florida. Undaunted by racism, the Sanchez family survived and loved America even as America at the time did not truly love and value them.

By the time Milo was born into a family of nine children, the bloodline and language of his ancestors was submerged through marriage and assimilation with their fellow Black Americans. His father drank heavily, and there were days when Milo ate at the homes of caring neighbors because there was no food at home. This early deprivation spurred a sturdy instinct for survival. It also ushered in a deep love for his mother, a woman who worked alongside her husband in the orange groves, which were plentiful in Florida. She would come home at the end of the day to wash clothes, clean her small house and feed her children. Money for food was always a problem, with her husband drinking up most of his pay or passing out in bars and having it stolen from him.

Against this backdrop of poverty and family dysfunction, there was the sting of racism. In 1952, the year Milo turned four, Jim Crow laws ruled the South. That same year his mother's cousin was lynched and dragged behind a car on the dirt road in front of Milo's home. Hearing a commotion and seeing the car in the distance as she stood in the front yard, Mrs. Sanchez quickly gathered her children and rushed them into the house, closing and locking the door behind her. The shades were pulled, and they sat—all of them, mother and children—in the semidarkness as the car with its cargo of hate and murder barreled down the dusty road. They waited unmoving until it had passed.

Milo grew up tough and resilient. He was an excellent student torn between working and attending school. He eventually missed so many days of school, working part-time, that the principal of the only Black high school in town expelled him. His teachers were sad to see him leave. They saw something in this young man who earned A's even with a poor attendance record.

But the poverty of his young life hurt him. He wanted nice clothes and decent shoes and money for cakes and sodas when he was hungry between meals. He got a job at an ice plant working for a man who it was said belonged to the Klu Klux Klan. He gave Milo a forty-hour week and never bothered him in any way. When Milo's friends were out partying and dancing on Friday nights, he worked at the ice plant. Some Saturdays he stopped by the teenage juke joint after work for a fish sandwich and soda. It was usually near closing time, and the crowd had thinned some. So it was quiet, and he was able to talk with a couple of friends.

He had no steady girlfriend during his teen years. The one girl he did like did not find him attractive. She thought his skin too black and his hair too kinky. There were other girls in his small community who found him attractive. But they were the daughters of men who taught school or owned small businesses. He felt too poor and socially unskilled to date them and become a part of their well-intentioned lives.

He joined the United States Marine Corps when he was eighteen years old and in service to his country found the purpose and discipline his young heart craved. For the first time in his life he experienced an abundance of food and came home looking like a man—broad-shouldered and well-muscled. He walked with a new grace, and the girls who had neglected him now wanted him. He was kind to them and enjoyed the attention, but there was something else on his mind. Vietnam. It wasn't the thought of being killed or wounded or far from home that bothered him. It was the thought of leaving his mother. He wouldn't be around to help care for his brothers and sisters. And for a while there would be no extra money to make her life easier.

He did survive the jungles of Vietnam—the war fought by teenagers barely nineteen years old, teenagers who were initiated into the horrors and vices of war and returned home unloved and not welcomed by their country. But Milo hid his hurt and disappointment at the cool reception his country extended to him upon his return. He braved the racial tension and civil unrest of those days and had no desire to join any protest or wage any social or political battles. The Black Panthers. The Nation of Islam. The NAACP. He was tired of fighting. He wanted rest. Quietness. And the thoughts of his own heart. After a summer's reunion with his family, he left Florida for Philadelphia. He wasn't content to spend his life in one place. A whole world had opened to him. In the Corps he met people from all over America. He flew in a plane for the first time and looked down at the city of Tokyo lit up at night. He watched the sun rise in Vietnam. He stood on a street in Los Angeles and watched people walk by. People of different nationalities and races. Brown. Black. White. Tan. Beautiful People. Americans.

CHAPTER TWO

One of the nurses who worked with Melita at the hospital talked often with her about life as a Christian—not in a pushy or forceful way but politely and with consideration. She also sensed Melita's need for friendship.

"Why don't you come to my church?" Takisha suggested. "Maybe you need a smaller church. Sometimes it's easier to make friends in a smaller church."

Melita didn't want to leave her church, but she did want friends. So she visited the church and found it to be a warm and welcoming place with interesting sermons and wonderful music. But a few months into their deepening friendship Takisha decided to move to North Carolina. She planned to marry her boyfriend and take a nursing job there. Melita was sad to have her leave.

"I want you to call my friend Milo." Takisha handed her a slip of paper. "He's a good person to talk with if you have any questions about your spiritual life. He's a Christian and one of my best friends. A good brother. I'm leaving, but God will send you another friend."

"I hope so." Melita smiled a little, and Takisha hugged her and said goodbye. At the end of her shift Melita took the paper out of her pocket and looked at it. Takisha had written a phone number for Milo Sanchez.

When she did call Milo, their conversation was an exchange of general information—names, occupations, birthplaces, number of years in Philadelphia, and how they both came to know Takisha. He also invited her to church. It was a date Melita missed after hurting her back at work. She was put on bed rest for three days and prescribed a medication that made her drowsy.

When Milo didn't see her at church (she had described what she would wear), he phoned. "What happened?" he asked.

"I hurt my back at work."

"Who's taking care of you?" He seemed concerned.

"No one. I'm okay. I can move without too much pain. I'm taking medicine, and I have to see a physical therapist if bed rest doesn't make me feel better."

"If you need anything, let me know, okay?"

"I will. Thank you."

"I'll call again to check on you. Is this all right?" he asked.

"Yes. Thank you." He kept his word and called every night until Melita was able to return to work.

CHAPTER THREE

As quiet entered Melita's life, malice seemed to leave Ruby's. She rehashed her divorce proceedings with Melita and began to dismiss eleven years of married life. Of the two women, Ruby was the more socially aggressive and continued to spend Saturday nights at clubs and lounges. She continued meeting men, but her interest in them was only superficial and temporary. Occasionally a man would express a real desire to involve himself in a relationship, but Ruby would find a way to get rid of him. She even tried to pass these men off on Melita, who had the good sense to refuse her offers.

One evening Ruby invited her to a lounge frequented by Jamaican Americans. Melita was reluctant to go, but Ruby begged her, and she went. The lounge was a happy, upbeat place. Melita met a man who sat and talked with her for most of the evening and asked to see her again when she and Ruby were ready to leave.

"The Tall Ships are coming to Philadelphia," Melita suggested. "I'd like to see them."

"When?" he asked.

"Tomorrow."

"That's kind of soon," he replied.

Melita wrote her phone number down and gave it to him. "Call me before two if you want to go."

"I don't have to beg him for a date," she told Ruby when they were outside. Ruby laughed. "This is the last lounge date I'm going on with you. From now on if it's not a concert, a ballet, or a play don't ask me."

"Why?" Ruby wondered.

"I'm tired of this. I want to get married. I want a family. And all these men want to do is play games and have sex. You've been married. You've had a husband, and you have children. Don't ask me to go to any more bars and lounges. The answer is no." Her voice had risen.

"Why are you mad at me?" Ruby asked.

"I'm not mad at you." Melita explained. "I'm just through wasting my time like this." They got into the car and drove off.

Melita felt as if she was approaching the end of something. She had started spending her evenings at home reading her Bible, which created an inner quietness in her. She was unwilling to have this peaceful quietness interrupted by any intense attachment to a man. As she read her Bible, she remembered things her mother had taught her about Jesus, and she realized He really was the son of God. He had died a bloody death on a wooden cross to free her from sin and hell. And He really did come back to life after dying on that cross. She believed this.

Jesus conquered death—all kinds of death. The death of hope. The death of innocence. He conquered loss too and loneliness and heartbreak. She could never be lost to Him or rejected by Him. He loved her.

Thinking of Jesus this way made Him personal to Melita. And

in a moment known at creation her heart was consumed with a desire to be forgiven for all her sins and wrongdoing. And she asked for this forgiveness and knew her life would never be the same because she was loved and forgiven by Him. This sense of a new beginning filled her whole being and made her feel clean and free and new.

CHAPTER FOUR

The young man Melita met at the lounge didn't call the next day, but Milo did. "What are you doing today?" he asked.

"I planned to see the Tall Ships down at Penn's Wharf, but my date hasn't called."

"Well, I'm going there too, and I want you to go with me."

"You do?"

"I'll tell you what. I'm in the neighborhood and I planned to stop by. If you're not home when I get there, it's okay. If you're at home, maybe we can go together."

"Okay."

A whole hour passed, and there was no phone call from the lounge lizard. When Milo buzzed her apartment, Melita walked out of the building and saw two men standing near the entrance. "Which one of you is Milo Sanchez?" she cautiously asked. Milo pointed to the man beside him. Melita looked appraisingly at the man and extended her hand.

"I am," Milo said then and laughed gently. Secretly Melita was very pleased as the other man walked away. She turned to Milo and his magnificent Blackness, taking in his height and broad shoulders. A feeling of relaxed happiness filled her. There was something brotherly about his joking with her. "I finally get to see you," he said and took her hand in his. "I used to live in this neighborhood. I ran a group home for seven boys."

"I've been here for a year," Melita offered. They began to walk down the avenue to the train station. Milo had an effortless charm, and Melita sensed no hidden agenda in him as he talked about himself. She was relieved to meet a man who talked about himself and let her listen. He said things that made her smile. She even looked down at his shoes, which were unfashionably pointed, and at the cuffs of his pants, which were too long. But none of this mattered. She liked his voice. It was full of good things.

The Tall Ships were impressive with their huge, billowing sails. They had come from as far away as Spain. The harbor was full of people enjoying the sunny weather and clear skies. The two of them walked along looking at the ships and came to a large crowd. Milo stepped in front of Melita and held her hand behind him as he guided her through. She looked up at his beautiful broad shoulders and felt shielded, protected. He stepped aside as the crowd thinned. "Look." He pointed at a blimp sailing overhead. "I remember seeing those when I was a kid. They haven't changed much. Look over there. See that?" Melita shielded her eyes from the sun. "It's the Moshulu. There's a restaurant inside. Let's go."

They walked to the ship and went inside to first examine its outfitting, and then Milo found a small table near a window, and they sat down. "Since we're here, we might as well order something," he said. "What would you like?"

"Something to drink."

"Is that all?"

"Yes."

He motioned to the waiter, who presented menus. Melita chose a tall lemonade and Milo a dish of ice cream. He offered Melita a spoonful. "How is it?" he asked. "I think it has alcohol in it." Milo tasted the ice cream and made a face. "They can't make anything these days without putting alcohol in it." He tasted another spoonful and put his spoon down. "Oh, well." He leaned back in his chair.

Melita noticed his left eye seemed to be a little off center. "You're probably wondering about my eye."

"I'm sorry. I didn't mean to stare." Melita felt embarrassed.

"You weren't staring. My dad drank, and sometimes he slapped me around. I had a doctor look at it, and he told me it was from an old injury to the muscle. I was in the military too, and I used to box, so it might have been the boxing that did it. Either one." Melita looked down at the table and felt sad for him. "What about your family?" he asked.

"My dad is alive, but my mom died not too long ago. I have three brothers, and they live with my dad. They're teenagers."

"So you're here alone? No relatives?"

"I have cousins here, but I'm not close to them. I don't know where they live either."

"Do you have friends here?"

"I have one." Milo thought a deep reserve of strength must lie hidden within her. How could a young woman—a kid almost— leave home to live in a city alone without family? There was something about her that made Milo feel protective. He watched her looking at him. Seeing him. His heart warmed.

Milo took her home and, once inside her apartment, sat in a chair across the room from her. He sat relaxed and at ease as if he had no place else to go and simply visited with her. The room seemed to grow brighter now that he was there.

They talked for a while, and then he asked her, "What do you want?"

"What do I want?"

"From life."

"A good job. Family. Home. All the usual things. Why do you ask?"

"Because I want to pray with you. And are you sure there's nothing else?" He smiled knowingly.

"Well, of course I'd like a nice boyfriend. Somebody I could spend time with going places and doing things together."

"It sounds like you need a friend. Let's pray and ask God to send you a friend. Is that okay?"

"Yes." The two of them stood up and approached one another to hold hands. Milo prayed in his even, clear voice, and Melita felt comforted. When they finished praying, he looked at his watch. "It's getting late, and I have church tomorrow morning. Look, I know you have your own church, but some Sunday morning would you like to visit with me?"

"Yes. I'd like that."

"Okay. It's a date then."

She walked him down the stairs, and they stood outside the apartment entrance. Milo looked up at the evening sky, now a pale pink touched with gold, and Melita followed his gaze. And when her eyes were lifted to the sky, Milo looked down at her standing there, her face full of the evening sun. He knew in that moment she was the woman he wanted with him as he lived out the rest of his life. And at that moment she looked up at him and smiled.

"You know," he suggested, "we could have a pretty nice time if you don't run away from me."

"Where would I go?" Melita asked.

"I don't know. You might go back home and leave Philadelphia."

"Why would I? I left everything to come here."

"I'll call you." He touched her hand. "Tomorrow at one." Melita watched him walk all the way down the avenue until he was out of sight. And the next day Milo called at one. And Melita was there to answer.

ABOUT THE AUTHOR

Rosa Bailey is passionate about creating Christian fiction that is relevant and true to modern life. *Leaving Yesterday* is her debut novel.

Printed in the United States
by Baker & Taylor Publisher Services